Greenwillow
Read-alone

Mrs. Gaddy and The Ghost

by WILSON GAGE
pictures by MARYLIN HAFNER

GREENWILLOW BOOKS
A Division of William Morrow & Company, Inc., New York

Library of Congress Cataloging in Publication Data
Steele, Mary Q.   Mrs. Gaddy and the ghost.   (Greenwillow read-alone)
Summary: Mrs. Gaddy finds a ghost in the kitchen can be good company.
[1. Ghost stories] I. Hafner, Marylin. II. Title. PZ7.S8146Mk [E]
78-16366. ISBN 0-688-80179-X ISBN 0-688-84179-1 lib. bdg.

For Libby, with affection
and with thanks • W.G.

For Abigail and Douglas,
with love • M.H.

Mrs. Gaddy was a farmer.

She had a little old house

and a big old barn.

She had some fields of corn

and a vegetable garden.

She had a meadow

and some apple trees.

She had a storm cellar to go in

if a tornado happened.

She had some chickens.

She had a cow and a mule.

It was a very nice farm.

There was only one trouble.

The little old house

was haunted.

There was a ghost in the kitchen.

It made awful noises at night.

Mrs. Gaddy did not like it.

She worked very hard.

She needed lots of sleep.

The ghost kept her awake.

She could not think

of any way to get rid

of that ghost.

7

One night Mrs. Gaddy

was sleeping.

Suddenly there was

a loud noise.

Thump! Thump! Thump!

Mrs. Gaddy woke up.

"Drat," she said.

"There is that ghost again.

Something must be done."

Mrs. Gaddy jumped out of bed.

She lighted her candle

and went downstairs.

She went in the kitchen

and looked all around.

"Come out!" she called.

"I know you're here.

I heard you thump!"

11

There was a ghosty-looking thing
high up in a corner of the kitchen.
Mrs. Gaddy got her broom
and swept it down.
She opened the back door and
swept the ghosty thing outside.
"There," she said.
"That takes care of that!"
And she went back to bed.

But a few nights later
she heard another noise.
Whooo! Whooo! Whooo!
"Drat and double drat!"
cried Mrs. Gaddy.
"That ghost has come back."
She took her candle
and went downstairs.
"Now it is in the chimney,"
she said.
She got some bug spray.

She sprayed and sprayed
up the chimney.
"There," she said.
"That ought to get rid of it!"
And she went back to bed.

But two nights later

she heard another noise.

Clank! Clank! Clank!

"Oh, my stars!" she yelled.

"That ghost has got in the oven!"

Mrs. Gaddy ran downstairs.

"I'll fix it now," she said.

She got a lot of wood

and built a big fire in the stove.

Then she sat down to wait.

She wanted to be sure

that ghost was really cooked.

"What a nice hot fire," she said.

"I should bake some bread."

Mrs. Gaddy went to the pantry.

There was her fresh bread

rising in the pans.

She forgot about the ghost.

She brought the pans
from the pantry and
opened the oven door.
Poof!

"Oh, tarnation!" Mrs. Gaddy shouted.
"I have let that ghost out!
  And what am I doing baking bread
  in the middle of the night?"
  She put the pans back in the pantry
  and went upstairs to bed.

20

The next night she heard
another awful noise.
Clump! Clump! Clump!
Mrs. Gaddy jumped out of bed
and ran down to the kitchen.
She held up her candle.

She thought she saw
something ghosty under the table.
She took off her slipper
and slapped the ghosty thing.
"Dang, I missed it," she said.

She slapped something ghosty
under her rocking chair.
"Missed again," said Mrs. Gaddy.

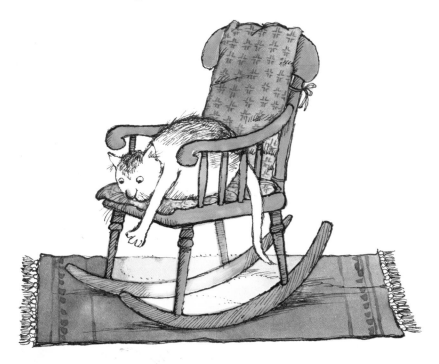

She slapped all around the kitchen.
"I will never hit that ghosty thing,"
she said. "It is too hard to see."

Suddenly something ghosty

jumped in the churn!

"Bless my soul!" Mrs. Gaddy cried.

"I have that ghost now!"

Quick as a flash she put

the lid on the churn.

She fastened the lid down tight.

"Good," said Mrs. Gaddy.

"It will never get out

of that churn."

And she went back to bed.

The next day Mrs. Gaddy got up early.

She fed her chickens.

She fed the mule.

"I must make my butter,"
said Mrs. Gaddy.
She got a pan of cream.
"Oh, my stars and garters!"
she hollered.
"That ghost is in my churn.
I need butter.
I will just have to
let the ghost out."

Mrs. Gaddy took the lid off the churn
and looked inside.

There was nothing there.

"Good gravy!" she cried.

"That ghost has got out
all by itself!"

Mrs. Gaddy was
really mad.
She poured
the cream
into the churn
and began
to churn it.

"I wish that ghost was still
in there," she said.
"I would churn it into bits.
I would make butter out of it
and feed it to my hens."

Suddenly she had an idea.
"I will set a trap for it,"
she said. "I will set
a mousetrap. I will use
gingerbread for bait.
Everybody likes gingerbread."

That night Mrs. Gaddy

set her mousetrap very carefully.

She used gingerbread for bait.

Then she went to bed.

She slept all night.

There were no scary noises.

Next morning Mrs. Gaddy
was very happy.
"Oh, I have caught
that ghost," she said.
She went downstairs.
The trap had been sprung.
The gingerbread was gone.
But there was nothing
in the trap.
"That ghost has got away
again!" she yelled.
"Whatever shall I do?"

Mrs. Gaddy thought and thought.
"I could spread glue
all over everything," she said.
"The glue would surely
catch the ghost.

But bless my big toe!
It would catch me too.
That would never do."
She thought some more.

"I could move away," she said.
"Oh, I would not like that.
I have lived here a long time.
I love my little old house
and my big old barn.
I would miss my apple trees
and my chickens and my cow.
Oh dear, oh dear."

FOR
SALE
CALL 354-0696

Mrs. Gaddy was very upset.

Still she had all her work to do.

She went out to the barn

to take care of her animals.

The barn was very tidy.

There were no rats or mice.

Mrs. Gaddy had an idea.

"Maybe I can get rid of that ghost

the way my grandmother

taught me to get rid

of rats and mice,"

she cried. "I will try it!"

Mrs. Gaddy ran back into her house.

She got her pen and some ink

and some paper.

She wrote a letter.

It was a very polite letter.

Dear Ghost,

Please go away and haunt some other house. There are many nice houses in this neighborhood.

Respectfully.

(Mrs.) Hilda Gaddy.

That night she put the letter
on the kitchen table.
"That ghost will be sure
to see it there," she said.
Then she went to bed
and fell fast asleep.

But something waked her
in the night.
Strange sounds were coming
from the kitchen.
"Oh, good gravy," she said.
"That ghost is crying!
What sad sounds!
Why is it crying like that?"
Mrs. Gaddy thought a minute.
"Oh, forevermore!
What have I done?"
she asked herself.

"That ghost has lived here
longer than I have.
It feels just the way I do.
It loves this little house.

It does not want to leave.

It wants to stay right here

in its own home."

47

Mrs. Gaddy jumped out of bed

and ran downstairs.

"Don't cry, ghost," she called.

"You don't have to leave.

I will tear up the letter.

Tomorrow I will go to town

and buy some earmuffs.

I will wear them when I go to bed.

Then I won't hear

all that thumping and clanking."

The ghost sniffled and snuffled.

"There, there," said Mrs. Gaddy.

"I mean it. You can stay."

Mrs. Gaddy tore up the letter
and threw it in the stove.
Then she went back to bed.
The ghost was very quiet.

Next day Mrs. Gaddy went to town.

That night when she went to bed,

she put on the earmuffs.

She could not hear a thing.

Late in the night
Mrs. Gaddy woke up.
Still she did not hear a thing.
She tossed and turned.
She counted sheep.
She couldn't get back to sleep.
Finally she sat up
and took off the earmuffs.
She could hear noises
in the kitchen.
Thump! Thump! Thump!

"What a nice noise,"
said Mrs. Gaddy.
"A ghost in the kitchen
is very good company.

Tomorrow I will bake
some gingerbread for it.
And now I believe
I can go back to sleep."
And she did.

WILSON GAGE is the pen name of Mary Q. Steele, who has written many popular books for children. As Wilson Gage she is the author of *Squash Pie* and *Down in the Boondocks*, both ALA Notable Books. Under her own name she is the author of *Journey Outside*, a Newbery Honor Book, as well as many other books, including *The Owl's Kiss*, *The True Men*, *The First of the Penguins*, and *Because of the Sand Witches There*.

Born and raised in Tennessee, Ms. Steele lives there today in Signal Mountain with her husband William O. Steele, who is also a writer.

MARYLIN HAFNER studied at Pratt Institute and the School of Visual Arts in New York City, and in her early career did advertising illustration and fabric design. She continues to do editorial illustrations for leading magazines and has illustrated many distinguished books, including *Mind Your Manners* by Peggy Parish, *It's Halloween* by Jack Prelutsky, *Camp KeeWee's Secret Weapon* and *Jenny and the Tennis Nut* by Janet Schulman, and *The Mango Tooth* by Charlotte Pomerantz.

Ms. Hafner lives in Cambridge, Massachusetts.